21st Century [

Hurricane Katrina

by Sue Gagliardi

F⦿CUS
READERS

BEAC⦿N

www.focusreaders.com

Focus Readers is distributed by North Star Editions:
sales@northstareditions.com | 888-417-0195

Produced for Focus Readers by Red Line Editorial.

Photographs ©: David J. Phillip/AP Images, cover, 1, 21; Jim Reed/RGB Ventures/SuperStock/Alamy, 4; FEMA/Alamy, 6; Vincent Laforet/UPI/Newscom, 9; lavizzara/Shutterstock Images, 10; AMFPhotography/Shutterstock Images, 13; Red Line Editorial, 15; Gerald Herbert/AP Images, 16–17; Lieut. Commander Mark Moran, NOAA Corps, NMAO/AOC/NOAA, 18; Eric Gay/AP Images, 22, 29; Patricia Marroquin/Shutterstock Images, 24; Carlos Barria/Reuters/Newscom, 26

Library of Congress Cataloging-in-Publication Data
Names: Gagliardi, Sue, 1969- author.
Title: Hurricane Katrina / by Sue Gagliardi.
Description: Lake Elmo, MN : Focus Readers, [2020] | Series: 21st century
   disasters | Audience: Grades 4-6. | Includes index.
Identifiers: LCCN 2019004532 (print) | LCCN 2019006771 (ebook) | ISBN
   9781641859479 (pdf) | ISBN 9781641858786 (ebook) | ISBN 9781641857406
   (hardcover) | ISBN 9781641858090 (pbk.)
Subjects: LCSH: Hurricane Katrina, 2005--Juvenile literature. |
   Hurricanes--Gulf States--Juvenile literature. |
   Hurricanes--Louisiana--Juvenile literature.
Classification: LCC HV636 2005.U6 (ebook) | LCC HV636 2005.U6 G34 2020
   (print) | DDC 976/.044--dc23
LC record available at https://lccn.loc.gov/2019004532

Printed in the United States of America
Mankato, MN
May, 2019

About the Author

Sue Gagliardi writes fiction, nonfiction, and poetry for children. Her books include *Fairies, Get Outside in Winter,* and *Get Outside in Spring*. Her work appears in children's magazines including *Highlights Hello, Highlights High Five, Ladybug,* and *Spider*. She teaches kindergarten and lives in Pennsylvania with her husband and son.

Table of Contents

Chapter 1

Water Rising

A huge storm woke the people of New Orleans, Louisiana. It was the morning of August 29, 2005. Strong winds swept through the city. Trees fell on houses and cars. Heavy rain pounded the ground.

Hurricane Katrina pounded the US coast with wind and rain.

 After the storm, deep water filled streets and buildings.

Soon, water filled the streets. Much of the city flooded. New Orleans had been hit by Hurricane Katrina.

Hurricanes are huge storms. Their spinning clouds bring strong winds and heavy rain. Hurricanes form over the ocean. But they can travel toward land. When hurricanes reach the shore, they cause major damage. Flooding can last for days.

Hurricane Katrina formed over the Atlantic Ocean. It started near the Bahamas, an island nation. Then it moved toward the Gulf Coast.

Did You Know?

By August 30, approximately 80 percent of New Orleans was underwater.

The Gulf Coast is made up of five states. They are Texas, Louisiana, Mississippi, Alabama, and Florida. Hurricane Katrina swept through this area.

Strong winds shattered windows and ripped roofs off houses. Floods covered huge areas of land.

Did You Know?

Scientists give a name to each major storm. The first one of the year starts with an A. The others go in alphabetical order. But they skip Q, U, X, Y, and Z.

 Water rushed past barriers and flooded whole neighborhoods.

Hundreds of people were hurt or killed. Thousands more were left searching for food and shelter.

Chapter 2

Understanding Hurricanes

Hurricanes form over warm ocean water. The air above the water warms and rises. Cool air replaces it. The water heats this air, too.

As more warm air rises, huge clouds form. The clouds spin.

As Hurricane Katrina neared land, its clouds were 415 miles (668 km) across.

As the storm grows, wind speeds increase. When wind speeds reach 74 miles per hour (119 km/h), the storm is called a hurricane.

A hurricane has three main parts. The eye is a calm area at the storm's center. The **eyewall** surrounds the eye. This part of the storm is made up of thick clouds. It has strong winds and rain. Rain bands spin out from the eyewall. These long, curved lines of clouds bring heavy rain. They can

 A hurricane's wind can flatten houses and fling cars.

stretch hundreds of miles from the

hurricane's eye.

As a hurricane moves near land, it

creates a huge wave of ocean water.

This wave is called the storm surge. Water from the rain and storm surge can cause **flash floods**.

Scientists rate a hurricane's **sustained** wind speed on a scale of one to five. These ratings are called categories. Storms with faster winds have higher numbers. These

Did You Know?

In some places, Hurricane Katrina's storm surge was more than 25 feet (7.6 m) high.

HURRICANE KATRINA TIMELINE

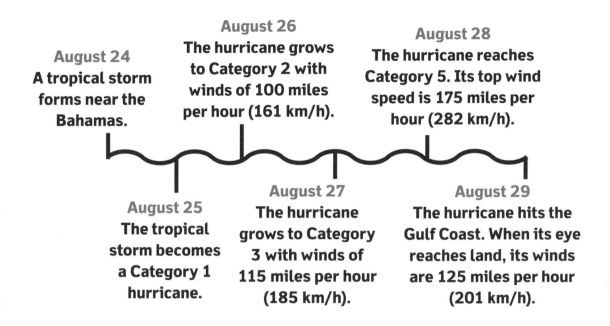

August 24
A tropical storm forms near the Bahamas.

August 26
The hurricane grows to Category 2 with winds of 100 miles per hour (161 km/h).

August 28
The hurricane reaches Category 5. Its top wind speed is 175 miles per hour (282 km/h).

August 25
The tropical storm becomes a Category 1 hurricane.

August 27
The hurricane grows to Category 3 with winds of 115 miles per hour (185 km/h).

August 29
The hurricane hits the Gulf Coast. When its eye reaches land, its winds are 125 miles per hour (201 km/h).

storms also cause more damage. At one point, Hurricane Katrina reached Category 5. But by the time its eye hit the Gulf Coast, it had slowed to Category 3.

Hurricanes

Winds and water from a hurricane can damage homes. To prepare, people should secure doors and windows. Outdoor items should be tied down or removed. Cities near coasts may build **levees** and **floodwalls**. These barriers hold back water.

However, **evacuating** is the best way to stay safe. People who live near coasts should listen for weather updates. If a hurricane is moving toward a city, experts may tell people to evacuate. People should leave right away. They should bring enough food and water for at least three days.

People build walls to protect homes from floodwaters.

Chapter 3

Survivor Stories

Seven-year-old Dillion Chancey was asleep when Hurricane Katrina hit. He woke to water rushing into his home in Mississippi.

Dillion and his parents climbed to the roof. The water kept rising.

 Thousands of homes flooded as a result of Hurricane Katrina.

They swam to their neighbor's house. But that house filled with water, too. Dillion and his parents jumped into the water. They floated on furniture and clung to trees.

Dillion and his parents drifted for 13 hours. Huge waves washed around them. Finally, they found

Did You Know?

In Louisiana, more than 1.5 million people evacuated before Hurricane Katrina hit.

> Helicopters rescued people who became stuck on the roofs of buildings.

dry land. But after the storm, their house was a pile of **debris**.

In New Orleans, thousands of residents became **stranded**. Many people did not have food or water.

Volunteers use boats to rescue stranded residents in New Orleans.

People in Lafayette, Louisiana, decided to help. They gathered nearly 400 boats. They made the two-hour trip to New Orleans. They used the boats to rescue more than 10,000 stranded people.

After the storm, thousands of people gathered inside the Superdome. This football stadium became a shelter during Hurricane Katrina. Nearly 30,000 people stayed there. Supplies of food and water ran low.

Did You Know?

After the hurricane, more than 250,000 people stayed in rescue shelters.

Chapter 4

After the Hurricane

Hurricane Katrina destroyed thousands of homes. The strong winds and flooding wiped out whole neighborhoods. Many people worked together to clean up and rebuild.

 Parts of New Orleans still hadn't been repaired 10 years later.

 New Orleans built a huge barrier along the coast to protect residents from future hurricanes.

Even so, some neighborhoods had no power for months after the storm. Other areas never recovered. People who lived in those areas had to find new homes.

Scientists work to **predict** hurricanes. They study the ocean. They look for places where storms are likely to form. If a storm does form, scientists track it. They measure where it moves and how fast it goes. That way, they can warn people in its path.

Did You Know?

Some aircraft can fly into a hurricane's eye. They measure temperature and wind speed.

FOCUS ON
Hurricane Katrina

Write your answers on a separate piece of paper.

1. Write a paragraph describing how a hurricane forms.

2. What do you think is the best way to prepare for a hurricane? Why?

3. What are the three main parts of a hurricane?
   - **A.** floodwall, levee, debris
   - **B.** eye, eyewall, rain bands
   - **C.** eyewall, floodwall, flood

4. What might happen when the eye of the hurricane passes over an area?
   - **A.** The area will get heavy rain.
   - **B.** The area will become very windy.
   - **C.** The area will have calm weather.

5. What does **major** mean in this book?

*When hurricanes reach the shore, they cause **major** damage. Flooding can last for days.*

    A. not very much

    B. very good

    C. very bad

6. What does **recovered** mean in this book?

*Other areas never **recovered**. People who lived in those areas had to find new homes.*

    A. traveled to a different place

    B. returned to normal after a problem

    C. filled with water after a storm

Answer key on page 32.

Glossary

debris
The remains of something broken.

evacuating
Leaving a place of danger.

eyewall
A ring of tall clouds that swirl around a hurricane's eye.

flash floods
Sudden rushes of water caused by heavy rain.

floodwalls
Walls built from concrete to stop floodwaters.

levees
Walls built from earth materials to stop floodwaters.

predict
To guess or estimate what might happen in the future.

stranded
Stuck in a place with no way to leave, especially a place of danger.

sustained
Lasting for a long period of time.

To Learn More

BOOKS

Abdo, Kenny. *How to Survive a Hurricane*. Minneapolis: Abdo Publishing, 2019.

Bell, Samantha S. *Detecting Hurricanes*. Lake Elmo, MN: Focus Readers, 2017.

Murray, Julie. *Hurricanes*. Minneapolis: Abdo Publishing, 2018.

NOTE TO EDUCATORS

Visit **www.focusreaders.com** to find lesson plans, activities, links, and other resources related to this title.

Index

A
Atlantic Ocean, 7

C
categories, 14–15
clouds, 6, 11–12

E
evacuate, 16, 20
eye, 12–13, 15, 27
eyewall, 12

F
flooding, 6–8, 14, 25
floodwalls, 16

G
Gulf Coast, 7–8, 15

L
levees, 16

N
New Orleans, Louisiana,
    5–7, 21–22

R
rain bands, 12

S
storm surge, 14

W
wind speeds, 12,
    14–15, 27